D1270885

TOP 10 DUNKERS IN BASKETBALL

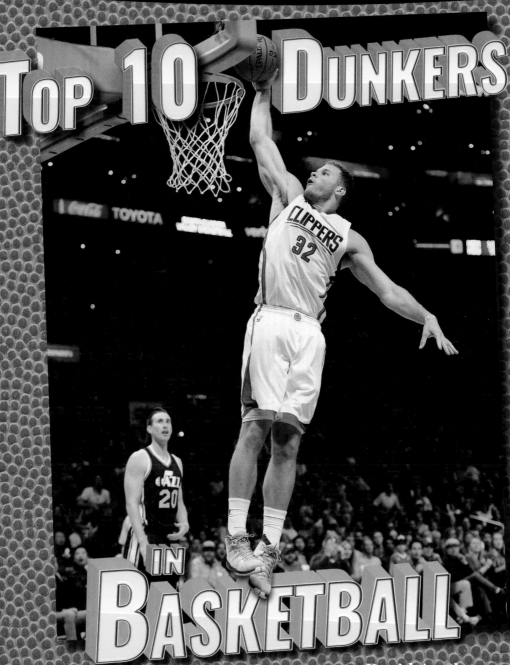

David Aretha

Enslow Publishing
101 W. 23rd Street
Suite 240
New York, NY 10011
USA
enslow.com

Published in 2017 by Enslow Publishing, LLC.
101 W. 23rd Street, Suite 240, New York, NY 10011

Library of Congress Cataloging-in-Publication Data

Names: Aretha, David.
Title: Top 10 dunkers in basketball / David Aretha.
Other titles: Top ten dunkers in basketball
Description: New York : Enslow Publishing, 2017. | Series: Sports Greats | Includes bibliographical references and index.
Identifiers: LCCN 2015051240| ISBN 9780766075849 (Library Bound) | ISBN 9780766075801 (Paperback) | ISBN
 9780766075825 (6-pack)
Subjects: LCSH: Dunking (Basketball)—Juvenile literature. | Basketball players—Rating of—United States—Juvenile literature.
Classification: LCC GV888.15 A74 2017 | DDC 796.323—dc23
LC record available at http://lccn.loc.gov/2015051240

Printed in the United States of America

To Our Readers: We have done our best to make sure all website addresses in this book were active and appropriate when we went to press. However, the author and the publisher have no control over and assume no liability for the material available on those websites or on any websites they may link to. Any comments or suggestions can be sent by e-mail to customerservice@enslow.com.

Photos Credits: Cover, p. 1 Harry How/Getty Images Sport/Getty Images; throughout book, Andrew Rich/E+/Getty Images (basketball texture background); pp. 5, 7, 8, 12 Manny Millan/Sports Illustrated/Getty Images; pp. 11, 27 © AP Images; p. 15 David E. Klutho /Sports Illustrated/Getty Images; p. 16 Kevin C. Cox/Getty Images Sport/Getty Images; p. 19 Stephen Dunn/ Allsport/Getty Images; p. 20 Mike Powell/Allsport/Getty Images; p. 23 BRIAN BAHR/AFP/Getty Images; p. 24 John Biever/ Sports Illustrated/Getty Images; p. 28 Darren McNamara/Allsport/Getty Images; p. 31 Jed Jacobsohn/Getty Images Sport/ Getty Images; p. 32 Jamie Squire/Getty Images Sport/Getty Images; p. 35 JAMES NIELSEN/AFP/Getty Images; p. 36 Greg Nelson /Sports Illustrated/Getty Images; p. 39 Robert Beck/Sports Illustrated/Getty Images; p. 40 Jeff Gross/Getty Images Sport/Getty Images; p. 43 TIMOTHY A. CLARY/AFP/Getty Images; p. 44 Elsa/Getty Images Sport/Getty Images.

★ CONTENTS ★

Introduction 4

Julius Erving 6

Darryl Dawkins 10

Dominique Wilkins. 14

Anthony Webb 18

Shawn Kemp 22

Vince Carter 26

Jason Richardson 30

Nate Robinson 34

Blake Griffin 38

Zach LaVine 42

Glossary 46

Further Reading 47

Index 48

When James Naismith invented a sport called basketball in 1891, he nailed a wooden basket ten feet off the ground. Ten feet. At that height, no player could possibly reach up and jam the ball through the basket. Or could they?

Naismith created the sport as a rainy-day activity inside a Springfield, Massachusetts, gymnasium. Basketball became so popular that a professional league was formed in 1898, and in 1936 it debuted as an Olympic sport in Berlin, Germany. That was where American Joe Fortenberry became the first known player to dunk in an organized game. *The New York Times* reported that the six-foot-eight Fortenberry could "pitch the ball downward into the hoop, much like a cafeteria customer dunking a roll in coffee."

Over the years, basketball attracted the tallest and most athletic men and women to the sport. Springy sneakers helped players jump even higher. Dunks became a common occurrence—so much so that the leaders of college basketball didn't like it. In 1967, the National Collegiate Athletic Association (NCAA) decided to ban the slam dunk. They felt it wasn't a skillful shot and gave super-tall players an unfair advantage. They also cited safety concerns.

From 1967 to 1976, no NCAA player was allowed to dunk. The ban frustrated fans of North Carolina State guard David "Skywalker" Thompson. Known for his amazing forty-eight-inch vertical leap, Thompson had to settle for boring layups. In his last college game, though, he cheated. On a fast break in front of his home crowd, Thompson threw down a spectacular dunk. "I got a technical foul and a standing ovation at the same time," he said.

Meanwhile, more and more pro players, such as forwards Connie Hawkins and Julius Erving, rocked arenas with slam dunks. In 1984–85, Chicago Bulls rookie guard Michael Jordan wowed the world with his high-flying jams. "It's got to be the shoes," said a character in Jordan's Nike shoe commercials. Soon, Nike was selling billions of dollars' worth of Air Jordan sneakers to kids who wanted to be "like Mike."

Jordan and fellow legends Kobe Bryant and LeBron James are three of the most sensational dunkers of all time. We did not feature them within these pages because they're profiled in another book in this series: *Top 10 Shooters and Scorers in Basketball*. We also considered other amazing jammers for this book, including Clyde "The Glide" Drexler and Dwight Howard. The six-foot-eleven, super-athletic Howard won the 2008 NBA Slam Dunk Contest while wearing a Superman cape.

In recent decades, players have turned the dunk into a celebration. Alley-oop, windmill, tomahawk, and 360 jams bring fans to their feet every time. The ten dunkers in this book are capable of all those slams and more. Darryl Dawkins shattered backboards with his dunks. Vince Carter hurdled a seven-foot Frenchman en route to a jam. And Blake Griffin once dunked over a car. It all has to be read to be believed.

Michael "Air" Jordan became world famous in the 1980s for his relentless scoring and gravity-defying dunks.

★ JULIUS ERVING ★

Nickname:	Dr. J
Teams:	Virginia Squires (ABA), 1971–1973
	New York Nets (ABA), 1973–1976
	Philadelphia 76ers, 1976–1987
Position:	Small forward
Height:	6'7"
Known for:	Aerial acrobatics

Julius Erving fondly recalled his first professional game back in the old American Basketball Association (ABA). Playing for the Virginia Squires, Erving drove to the basket with the league's red, white, and blue ball. As he soared high, he was guarded by two huge Kentucky Colonels. "I went in between both of them and just hung there and waited for them to come down. Then I dunked on them so hard I fell on my back," Erving told the *Boston Globe*. "Just doing that made me confident to go after anyone, anytime, anywhere, without any fear."

Classy, articulate, and highly respected, Dr. J was the biggest star of his era. He was the first professional player to perform nightly magic in midair. He could not only fly, he could also change directions while airborne. It was as if an invisible jet pack were strapped on his back.

In the 1980 NBA Finals for Philadelphia, Julius made one of the most amazing shots in league history. Against the Los Angeles Lakers, he drove along the baseline for a layup. But after leaving his feet, he realized that two players were blocking his path. So, with that invisible jet pack of his, he floated behind the backboard and came around to the other side of the basket. He flipped the ball off the glass for two points.

"Here I was, trying to win a championship, and my mouth just dropped open," recalled Lakers rookie Magic Johnson. "He actually did that. I thought, 'What should we do? Should we take the ball out or should we ask him to do it again?'"

Erving grew up in Long Island, New York. In high school, he called a buddy of his "Professor," and that kid called him

Julius Erving emerged as an American hero while starring in the ABA. The league's red, white, and blue ball, coupled with the New York Nets' American flag-like uniforms, added to the patriotic flair.

Erving skies against Kareem Abdul-Jabbar of the Los Angeles Lakers. Knowing Dr. J, he probably made another move or two before flipping the ball into the basket.

"Doctor." Dr. J became one of the most famous nicknames in American sports history.

Erving spent his first five professional seasons in the ABA, a league that rivaled the NBA from 1967 to '76. Julius won three ABA scoring titles and three MVP Awards, and he took the New York Nets to two ABA championships. With Philadelphia, he won the 1980–81 NBA MVP Award and led the 76ers to the 1983 league title. In all sixteen of his ABA/NBA seasons, he made the All-Star team and the playoffs.

Inside the Spectrum in Philadelphia, Dr. J brought fans to their feet with his majestic play. When he was especially hot, the announcer would shout, "The Doctor is op-erating!" Erving became the third player in ABA/NBA history, following Wilt Chamberlain and Kareem Abdul-Jabbar, to reach 30,000 points.

In the 1976 ABA Slam Dunk Contest in Denver, all competitors were required to take off from a ten-foot marker and dunk. For Dr. J, that was child's play. He launched himself from the free throw line—fifteen feet away—and jammed. He won the contest.

Eight years later, also in Denver, Erving competed in the very first NBA Slam Dunk Contest. Though he was nearly thirty-four years old, Julius still took off from the foul line and jammed. He finished second in the contest to Larry Nance, who—like a lot of players—had grown up idolizing Dr. J.

★ DARRYL DAWKINS ★

Nickname:	*Chocolate Thunder*
Teams:	*Philadelphia 76ers, 1975–1982; New Jersey Nets, 1982–1987; Utah Jazz, 1987; Detroit Pistons, 1987–1989*
Position:	*Center*
Height:	*6'11"*
Known for:	*Nicknaming his dunks*

Darryl Dawkins' dunks were so spectacular that even a blind man—musical artist Stevie Wonder—felt their impact. "Stevie Wonder used to come to ball games and they would have a guy sitting with him," Dawkins explained in *Dime* magazine. "And the guy would be holding on to his arm, telling him what's going on, and he would say, 'Hey, the big chocolate guy just put down a thunder dunk. The chocolate guy with another monster dunk.' And Stevie Wonder actually gave me the nickname Chocolate Thunder. So a guy who never saw me can give me that name."

Dawkins didn't need anyone's help when it came to nicknames. The big happy-go-lucky center called himself Sir Slam and Dr. Dunkenstein. And, he joked, he hailed from planet Lovetron. He even named his dunks—calling them the Rim Wrecker, the Yo-Mama, the Look Out Below, the Spine-Chiller Supreme, the In-Your-Face Disgrace, and the Cover Your Head.

Dawkins is lost amid the flying glass after shattering the backboard in Kansas City on November 13, 1979. Because of Darryl, the NBA worked at making backboards less breakable.

His teammates and opponents had to literally cover their heads on November 13, 1979. Darryl's Philadelphia 76ers were in Kansas City to play the Kings when all heck broke loose. The 250-pound giant rose over KC's Bill Robinzine and put his full weight into a jam. He tore the rim off the backboard and shattered the glass. Dawkins later called the dunk the If-You-Ain't-Groovin', Best-Get-Movin', Chocolate-Thunder-Flyin', Robinzine-Cryin', Teeth-Shakin', Glass-Breakin', Rump-Roastin', Bun-Toastin', Glass-Still Flyin', Wham-Bam-I-Am-Jam.

A few games later, Dawkins shattered another backboard. He called that one the Chocolate-Thunder-Ain't-Playin', Get-Out-Of-the-Wayin,' Backboard-Swayin', Game-Delayin' Super Spike.

Born in 1957, Darryl grew up in Orlando, Florida. At Maynard Evans High School, he impressed people with his friendly ways, big heart, powerful low-post game, and accurate shooting. In 1975, he became the first high school

Always the showman, Dawkins jammed in a variety of ways. Here, he stuffs the ball behind his head with his left hand.

player ever to be selected in the first round of the NBA Draft. For six years in Philadelphia, he teamed with legendary dunker Julius Erving.

Dawkins was a mediocre NBA center with an average of 12.0 points and 6.1 rebounds per game for his career. He relied on his power moves down low and his occasional outside shot. He admittedly did not listen to coaches' advice very well, and he never refined his moves around the basket.

Still, he left a colorful legacy. During one fast-break dunk against the Los Angeles Lakers, Dawkins knocked over forward Bob McAdoo. The poor opponent fell backward and flipped over. In another game, three Phoenix Suns surrounded the rim as they rose to rebound a missed 76ers shot. Racing out of nowhere, Darryl soared above the trio, snatched the ball with one hand, and jammed it through the iron.

Though he never reached his expectations, Dawkins delighted fans with his highlight-reel plays, flamboyant suits, and friendly nature. The basketball world mourned his loss when he died of a heart attack in 2015 at age fifty-eight. "We will always remember Darryl for his incredible talent, his infectious enthusiasm, and his boundless generosity," said NBA Commissioner David Silver. "He played the game with passion, integrity, and joy, never forgetting how great an influence he had on his legions of fans, young and old."

★ DOMINIQUE WILKINS ★

Nickname:	*The Human Highlight Film*
Teams:	*Atlanta Hawks, 1982–1994; Los Angeles Clippers, 1994; Boston Celtics, 1994–1995; San Antonio Spurs, 1996–1997; Orlando Magic, 1998–1999*
Position:	*Small forward*
Height:	*6'8"*
Known for:	*His dunk battle against Michael Jordan*

On February 9, 1985, millions of excited TV viewers tuned in to the NBA Slam Dunk Contest. Spectacular rookie Michael "Air" Jordan would face the league's most famous dunker, Dominique Wilkins, known as The Human Highlight Film.

Wilkins will never forget that epic showdown between him and MJ. "We wanted to win—at all costs," Wilkins said in a 2015 *Bleacher Report* interview. "The anticipation was so huge. So much hype. It set up for the perfect dunk contest."

Back then, the participants didn't use fancy props. In the semifinal round, Jordan simply stuck a piece of white tape on the free throw line. Famously, MJ took flight from that line and dunked, which earned a perfect score of 50. In the finals, he faced 'Nique.

"I always brought an element of flair and power to the dunk contest," Wilkins told *Bleacher Report*, and he was about to prove it. On his first final-round dunk, Wilkins bounced the ball off the

Wilkins scored 26,668 career points, including many on "video game dunks."

backboard, caught it, and flushed a two-handed reverse. On the next dunk, he nailed a ferocious two-handed windmill dunk. He scored a 50 on each and won the title. He won the contest again in 1990.

It's not surprising that Dominique's father was in the *Air* Force. Growing up in Baltimore and Washington, 'Nique flew high on the basketball courts. After a five-inch growth spurt prior to the tenth grade, he stood six-foot-eight. At that point, everyone knew he was destined for the NBA. Wilkins earned All-American honors at the University of Georgia, and he was drafted third overall by Utah in the 1982 NBA Draft. The Jazz traded him to Atlanta, where he thrilled fans for a dozen seasons.

The Hawks honor Dominique Wilkins with the unveiling of a statue in his name at Philips Arena on March 5, 2015.

"We were basically a football town," former Atlanta Mayor Andrew Young told NBA.com. "And Dominique was the first of the homegrown heroes that made us a basketball city. He filled the Omni [Center]. He was a superhero! He walked with such a bounce, it looked like he might take off with any step."

Wilkins averaged 26.4 points per game in his years with Atlanta and topped 30 PPG in 1985–86 and 1987–88. He made the All-Star Game nine consecutive seasons. He scored on fast breaks, midrange jumpers, and drives to the basket. His dunk repertoire, reported NBA.com, featured "double pump reverses, the one and two-handed windmills and sidewinders, the thunderous throw-downs over most every marquee player. There's a reason they call them 'videogame dunks.'"

Teammate Jon Koncak recalled the night Wilkins took a shot from the top of the key. "The ball hit the back of the rim and went straight up," Koncak told NBA.com. "The next thing I know, there are these arms grabbing the ball and dunking it. I was like, What the heck! He covered that distance, jumped above everybody, caught the ball and dunked it over three of us—two on his own team! I think even he was shocked that he could do that."

A friendly, approachable person, Wilkins helped support numerous local charities, including Big Brothers Big Sisters of Atlanta. In 2015, the Hawks honored 'Nique with a thirteen-foot statue outside Philips Arena.

"Cities need heroes," Young said. "And Dominique sure was ours for a long time."

Nickname:	**Spud Webb**
Teams:	**Atlanta Hawks, 1985–1991; Sacramento Kings, 1991–1995; Atlanta Hawks, 1995–1996; Minnesota Timberwolves, 1996; Orlando Magic, 1997–1998**
Position:	**Guard**
Height:	**5'7"**
Known for:	**Slaying the giants**

When an injured Michael Jordan couldn't compete in the 1986 NBA Slam Dunk Contest, the league asked Spud Webb to fill in for him. The five-foot-seven guard agreed—much to the amusement of his Atlanta Hawks teammates. They started teasing him about the dunks he should perform. One player thought it would be cute if he wore a cape with a big S on it.

"I remember thinking to myself, 'These guys are making a big joke out of this, but it isn't a joke,'" Webb wrote in his autobiography, *Flying High*. "I can do things they don't know about. None of these guys know what I can do."

Throughout his life, Anthony Webb had been disrespected. He got stuck with his nickname because a family friend thought his head was shaped liked the Soviet satellite *Sputnik*. Spud was so short that at age twelve, he and his friend played basketball *inside* the garage. When he wanted to play junior high hoops in Dallas,

Texas, his coach initially told him to go sit in the stands. At Wilmer-Hutchins High School, fellow coaches told the head coach he'd be a fool to play a "midget."

Division I schools were not interested in Webb, but he starred at both Midland Junior College and then North Carolina State. As a Hawks rookie in 1985–86, he brought quickness and slick passing off the bench. He also boasted a vertical leap of forty-two inches.

Reunion Arena in Dallas hosted the 1986 Slam Dunk Contest, and Spud was determined to shine in front of the hometown crowd. In the first round, he stunned the seventeen thousand fans—and millions on television—with a double-pump reverse jam and then a 360-degree flush. In a second-round dunk, he tossed the ball ahead on a high arc, caught it

Webb said, "I must have tried dunking over 1,000 times before I actually did it."

Spud climbs the ladder for a bucket during the 1987 Magic Johnson All-Star Game.

near the basket, twirled around, and flushed a reverse slam. All five judges held up 10-point cards, which resulted in a perfect score for the dunk.

Spud advanced to the third and final round against legendary dunker Dominique Wilkins—his Hawks teammate. Each would get two dunks. Because his life was turning around that day, he wrote, he opened with a 360-degree one-handed jam. It was extra amazing because his hand was too small to palm a basketball. Nevertheless, he executed it perfectly and earned a score of 50. Wilkins matched the score with 360 windmill slam.

For his grand finale, Webb lobbed the ball off the backboard, soared like *Sputnik*, caught the ball with one hand, and threw it down. Another 50! Spud beamed a huge smile as the crowd went wild. After Wilkins' final flush earned a 49, Spud Webb was declared the Slam Dunk champion.

The little guy went on to play twelve seasons in the NBA, including six as a starter. In 1991–92, he averaged 16.0 points and 7.1 assists per game for the Sacramento Kings. In 1994–95, he led the NBA in free throw percentage (.934). Yet he'll always be known for his giant performance in the 1986 Slam Dunk Contest.

"I don't play small," Webb said. "You have to go out and play with what you have. I admit I used to want to be tall. But I made it in high school, college, and now the pros. So it doesn't matter."

★ SHAWN KEMP ★

Nickname:	Reign Man
Teams:	Seattle SuperSonics, 1989–1997 Cleveland Cavaliers, 1997–2000 Portland Trail Blazers, 2000–2002 Orlando Magic, 2002–2003
Position:	Power forward
Height:	6'10"
Known for:	Arena-rocking power jams

It was Shawn Kemp's most spectacular dunk, but only a few people were there to witness it. The setting was a neighborhood basketball court in Elkhart, Indiana—Kemp's hometown. A teammate lobbed the ball high in the air and Shawn—flying in on a fast break—grabbed it with his left hand. While still in the air, he reversed his body 180 degrees and dropped an atomic dunk.

"He dunked the ball so hard, sparks flew off the metal-chain net on the basket," Shawn's cousin Kerry Ellison told *The Seattle Times*. "I realize things tend to get exaggerated over time, but you had to be there. And if you weren't there, you don't want to hear about it because you don't want to know what you missed."

Kemp jammed so hard during playground games that he often cut and bruised his wrists on the iron.

"You've got to stop dunking the ball so hard," Ellison would say.

"When I dunk," Shawn would reply, "I just want to tear the rim down."

Perhaps Kemp dunked out of frustration or anger. Shawn, the son of divorced parents, attended Concord High School in Elkhart. An African American kid in a mostly white school, Shawn did not do well in the classroom. As a senior, he failed to score 700 on his Standard Aptitude Test (SAT), which meant he was ineligible to play basketball as a college freshman. Opposing high school fans mocked him by chanting, "S-A-T! S-A-T!" After one game against rival Elkhart Central High School, opposing fans threw banana peels at him—an ugly, racist gesture.

Kemp spent time at the University of Kentucky and Trinity Valley Community College in Texas, but he did not play basketball at either school. Then, at age nineteen, he was selected by the Seattle SuperSonics in the 1989 NBA Draft.

For fourteen seasons, the uber-athletic power forward

Ferocious around the basket, Kemp ranks second in SuperSonics history in career rebounds and blocked shots—and, undoubtedly, first in slam dunks.

Shawn gets ready to rock the Charlotte Coliseum during the 1991 NBA Slam Dunk Contest. He made it to the contest's final round, where he lost to Boston's Dee Brown.

electrified NBA arenas with his dazzling dunks. In a game against the New York Knicks, Kenny "Sky" Walker leapt high to block a potential Kemp dunk. While in midair, Shawn twisted to the side of Walker and flushed a reverse jam. During other historic slams, Kemp knocked over Detroit's Bill Laimbeer and Golden State's Alton Lister like dominoes.

From 1992 through 1998, Shawn averaged 18.5 points and 10.5 rebounds per game and made the NBA All-Star Game each season. Though he was an average outside shooter, he was explosive on the fast break and scored with assorted moves around the basket.

Reign Man put on sensational shows in four NBA Slam Dunk Contests: 1990, '91, '92, and '94. He specialized in bouncing the ball high, catching it, and then finishing with a rim-shaking flush. He also perfected the windmill slam. While airborne, he held his right arm straight out and then wound it up toward the rim for the dunk.

Though he didn't win a Slam Dunk Contest, Kemp rates with Julius Erving and Dominique Wilkins as a jamming legend. In 2015, NBA.com ranked Shawn among the ten greatest dunkers in the history of the league.

★ VINCE CARTER ★

Nickname:	Vinsanity
Teams:	Toronto Raptors, 1998–2004; New Jersey Nets, 2004–2009; Orlando Magic, 2009–2010; Phoenix Suns, 2010–2011; Dallas Mavericks, 2011–2014; Memphis Grizzlies, 2014–present
Position:	Shooting guard
Height:	6'6"
Known for:	Poster-izing Frederic Weis

In September 2000, Vince Carter performed the greatest slam dunk ever in a basketball game. It was during the Olympics in Australia—USA vs. France. The French refer to it as *le dunk de la morte,* or the dunk of death. But we'll get to that dunk later. First, our discussion of Vince Carter should begin with his jam-aganza in the 2000 NBA Slam Dunk Contest.

Carter had starred at the University of North Carolina, Michael Jordan's alma mater. While MJ was nicknamed Air, VC became known as Air Canada after being drafted by the Toronto Raptors in 1998. With a vertical leap of forty-three inches, Carter dazzled the league with high-flying, head-spinning, rim-trembling jams.

Vince made his Slam Dunk Contest debut in 2000, and fans anxiously awaited his performance. He pulled off several amazing jams en route to victory, but two stand out. One was a reverse

360-degree windmill flush that rocked Oakland Arena. "I just said, I'm going to try it," he told *USA Today*. "I felt like I could jump to the moon. I pulled it off and I jumped higher than ever, and when I got around for that 360 and saw the rim, I just threw it through."

Next came the honey dip. Carter jammed the ball so deeply with his right hand that he hung onto the rim by the crook of his elbow. He continued to sway below the rim for two seconds while hysteria swept through the building.

The NBA Slam Dunk Contest had become rather dull in the mid-1990s, and it wasn't even held in 1998 and '99. But VC's electrifying performance in 2000 rejuvenated the event, which has become a thrilling celebration ever since.

From 2000 to '07, Carter made the All-Star team every year. He averaged more than 24 PPG in a season six times, and on February 27, 2000, he scored 51 points. Vinsanity exploded to the basket for points, and he rose so high on his jump shots that he had a clear view of the rim. He could also swish the long ball.

Carter earned NBA All-Star Game selections eight years in a row (2000–07), the last three of which were with the New Jersey Nets.

Vince leapfrogs France's Frederic Weis during the 2000 Olympics to make perhaps the greatest dunk in history. Note how far away he still is from the basket.

Entering the 2015–16 season, he ranked sixth in NBA history with 1,878 three-point field goals.

Though a tremendous all-around player, Carter will forever be known for his gravity-defying dunks. As mentioned, the greatest of all occurred in the 2000 Olympics. Vince stole the ball and charged toward the French basket. Standing in his way was opponent Frederic Weis. While Weis stood there like a statue, Carter decided to hurdle his foe's body—even though the Frenchman stood seven-foot-two! While airborne, VC split his legs wide and smacked Weis' head with his crotch. All the while, he reached far forward and stuffed the rock.

Carter celebrated with a howl, a leg shake, and a fist pump. As for Weis, "I learned people can fly."

"I knew he could jump, but I didn't know he could jump over me," Weis told reporters after the game. "Everybody will know my face now or my [jersey] number, at least. It's going to be on a poster, for sure."

He was right. To this day, posters of Vinsanity flying over Weis's head are available for purchase online.

★ JASON RICHARDSON ★

Nickname:	*J-Rich*
Teams:	*Golden State Warriors, 2001–2002; Charlotte Bobcats, 2007–2008; Phoenix Suns, 2008–2010; Orlando Magic, 2010–2012; Philadelphia 76ers, 2012–2013, 2014–2015*
Position:	*Shooting guard Height: 6'6"*
Known for:	*Winning back-to-back NBA Slam Dunk Contests*

In 2005, NBA.com asked fans to vote for the best Slam Dunk Contest jams of all time. Fans voted Michael Jordan's Kiss the Rim (1987) fifth best, and MJ's Free Throw Line Dunk (1988) ranked fourth. In third place came Vince Carter's Off-the-Floor and Between-the-Legs (2000). The top two dunks both belonged to Jason Richardson.

J-Rich pulled off the number two jam in 2004. Standing at the free throw line, he flipped the ball off the glass. He then grabbed the rebound while ascending, transferred the ball midair from his left hand to his right hand between his legs, and stuffed it. "Are you kidding me?!" screamed commentator Kenny Smith. "That's sick! That is sick! He's got the flu!"

Richardson didn't win the dunk title that year, but he did prevail as a rookie in 2002 and again in '03. As such, he became the third man to win consecutive NBA Slam Dunk Contests. Only Michael Jordan and Nate Robinson had done it before him.

In the 2003 Slam Dunk Contest, J-Rich threw down the number one dunk in the history of the event, according to the NBA.com poll. It was the final round, and Jason was feeling pressure. Desmond Mason had just flushed a sensational jam, and "I was like, man, I lost this dunk contest," J-Rich told NBA.com. Richardson would need perfect scores from the judges, and they wouldn't hand out 10s easily. One of the judges was Julius Erving, and another was Michael Jordan.

Commentators said that Jason would need the best dunk of his life to win this battle. Gilbert Arenas, Jason's Golden State teammate, suggested the jam he should try. J-Rich wasn't sure he could do it, but he made the attempt.

From the baseline, Jason bounced the ball high off the floor. While hanging in the air, he transferred the ball through his legs from right hand to left and stuffed a backward jam with his left hand. The crowd

Richardson performs his legendary dunk at the 2004 NBA All-Star Game. What made it special was that he passed the ball through his legs while ascending.

Here's the 2005 jam that NBA.com fans rated as the best Slam Dunk Contest stuff ever. While airborne, J-Rich passed the ball through his legs before dunking backward with his left hand.

at Philips Arena in Atlanta went wild, as did Kenny Smith. "I've seen something I've never seen before!" he yelled. NBA All-Stars came running onto the court.

"I kind of just looked at everybody to see what their reaction was," Richardson said in the NBA.com interview. "When I saw all the guys running out on the court, I was like, 'Yeah, this is a dunk [nobody] has done before.'"

Richardson enjoyed a terrific thirteen-year career in the NBA. The Michigan State alumnus averaged 17.1 points per game overall, and in three seasons he exceeded 20 PPG. With a forty-six-inch vertical leap—one of the greatest in league history—he dunked with ease. On fast breaks, he converted 360-degree stuffs and windmill jams like they were simple layups. He also became a prolific three-point shooter and led the NBA with 243 threes in 2007–08 for Charlotte.

Eventually, all the leaping took a toll on Jason's knees, and in 2015 he decided to retire. When Golden State won the NBA title that June, many fans at the victory parade were wearing Richardson jerseys even though he hadn't played with the team in eight years. Apparently, they still cherished his memorable dunks, including two of the greatest of all time.

Nickname:	Nate-Rob
Teams:	New York Knicks, 2005–2010; Boston Celtics, 2010–2011; Oklahoma City Thunder, 2011; Golden State Warriors, 2011–2012; Chicago Bulls, 2012–2013; Denver Nuggets, 2013–2015; Los Angeles Clippers, 2015; New Orleans Pelicans, 2015
Position:	Point guard
Height:	5'9"
Known for:	Three NBA Slam Dunk championships

It should have been an easy two points for Yao Ming. The Houston Rockets center raised his arms high and was about to release the ball toward the basket. But in a flash, New York's Nate Robinson blasted skyward. Though he was *twenty-one inches* shorter than Ming, Robinson rose to eye level with the Chinese giant and swatted the ball away. The Knicks crowd went berserk.

"That block surprised me because he's just so much taller than even other guys," Robinson told ThePostGame.com. "I just saw the play and I jumped, and I didn't have any fear and I made history."

Nate-Rob made a great deal of history in his ten-year NBA career. He is the only player to win three NBA Slam Dunk Contests, and he did so despite standing just five-foot-nine.

Robinson began dunking early in his high school career. Everybody on his team could dunk, and he was determined to do

Robinson skies over dunking legend Spud Webb for a jam in the 2006 NBA Slam Dunk Contest. All five judges held up their 10-point cards.

so. His first in-game slam came as a spectacular alley-oop flush—a seemingly impossible feat for a kid his size.

"First and foremost, you have to believe in yourself," Nate told ThePostGame.com. "You have to want it so bad that you just go out and work hard and get it. You can't have any fear."

A phenomenal athlete, Robinson starred in basketball, football, and track at Rainier Beach High School in Seattle, Washington. Despite his short legs and thick body, he has a vertical leap of forty-three inches. How can he jump so high? "So much of dunking

Dallas Cowboys cheerleaders—and even Nate himself—wave pompoms to celebrate his successful slam in the 2010 NBA Slam Dunk Contest.

comes from your core," he said in the same interview. "I do so many sit-ups and crunches and high knees and running the bleachers in the off-season because lots of jumping comes from ab muscles."

Kryptonate often showed off his skills at the NBA Slam Dunk Contest, and he won in 2006, '09, and '10. In the first affair, he dunked over five-foot-seven dunking legend Spud Webb for a perfect score of 50. In 2007, Knicks teammate David Lee held the ball high like a torch. Robinson leapt, plucked the ball off Lee's hand, and continued with a 360-degree dunk. On his way to victory in '09, he rose over six-foot-eleven Dwight Howard for a slam—then danced a little jig.

With the 2010 contest in Dallas, Robinson employed the services of several Dallas Cowboys cheerleaders for his grand finale. With the women cheering him on, Nate flung the ball off the backboard, grabbed it, and twirled midair for a two-handed backward jam. He celebrated by waving a cheerleader's pompoms.

In his career, Robinson averaged 11.0 points and 3.0 assists per game. Mostly, his role was to bring energy and hustle off the bench. In one game against Cleveland, he blocked the shot of legendary seven-footer Shaquille O'Neal and knocked the 350-pounder to the floor.

The way Nate played, it's as if someone forgot to tell him he was five-foot-nine. "God blessed me with a lot of heart and no height," he said, "and I'll take that any day."

★ BLAKE GRIFFIN ★

Nickname:	None
Teams:	Los Angeles Clippers, 2010–present
Position:	Power forward
Height:	6'10"
Known for:	Dunking over a Kia Optima

Blake Griffin, who grew up watching and rewatching the NBA's Slam Dunk Contests, was asked to compete in the event as a rookie in 2011. "When they first came to me . . . they said there were no rules," Griffin said. "I was like, 'So I can jump over a car? Yeah? Oh, maybe I have to do it now.'"

And so, in the final round of the 2011 contest, he did. A Kia Optima was driven onto the court of the Staples Center, home of Griffin's Los Angeles Clippers. Enhancing the drama, the Crenshaw Elite Choir gathered at the court and sang "I Believe I Can Fly." Clippers guard Baron Davis stood inside the Optima while holding a basketball with his head sticking through the sunroof. From there, Davis lobbed a high pass to Griffin, who soared over the hood of the car, caught the ball, and slammed it home. He hung onto the rim and then planted his feet on the car. The crowd went berserk.

Washington's Javale McGee, Griffin's competitor in the final round, knew he was doomed. "Nothing is going to beat that," McGee said, "unless I bring a plane out or something."

Griffin indeed won the contest. At season's end, he captured the NBA Rookie of the Year Award—due largely to his explosive dunks.

A composite photo illustration of multiple exposures shows how Griffin jammed over a Kia Optima to win the 2011 NBA Slam Dunk Contest.

Blake and his older brother Taylor grew up in Oklahoma City, Oklahoma. The NBA's Oklahoma City Thunder had yet to exist, so the Griffins made their own thunder on the court. Considering that their father, Tommy Griffin, coached basketball and owned a trophy company, the boys seemed destined for greatness. In high school, both were named their state's Player of the Year.

Taylor and Blake each starred at the University of Oklahoma and made the NBA. But only Blake—the number one overall pick

Blake often dunks with ferocity, as revealed in this photo. Note his rippling muscles, his determined expression, and how the ball fires like a bullet through the net.

in 2010—excelled in the league. Over his first five seasons, he averaged 21.5 points and 9.7 rebounds per game while making the NBA All-Star Game every year.

Amazingly athletic for six-foot-eleven, Griffin dunks with intensity—his face twisted into a snarl. His body is so long and his leaping ability so great that he can dunk on players while several feet from the basket. Such was the case against the Los Angeles Lakers on April 4, 2012. While Lakers seven-footer Pau Gasol leapt to rebound a missed Clippers shot, Griffin charged from behind, grabbed the rebound, and slammed over Gasol's head. Later in the game, Blake threw down a tomahawk jam over Gasol that knocked him to the floor for the second time.

Timofey Mozgov could feel Gasol's pain. On November 20, 2010, Griffin rose so high on the seven-foot-one New York Knicks center that Blake's waistband was in Mozgov's face. Griffin rested his left hand on the Russian's head while slamming ferociously.

Blake has become so famous for his dunks that NBA player Metta World Peace said he looked forward to being his victim. "I'm not going to lie," he said. "I hope he dunks on me, puts his shoulders on my face, and, like, Aaaaah!"

If he can leap over an Optima, he can do the same to Metta. Only in the NBA. . . .

★ ZACH LaVINE ★

Nickname: None
Teams: Minnesota Timberwolves, 2014–present
Position: Point guard
Height: 6'5"
Known for: His *Space Jam* jam

Around the age of five, Zach LaVine was inspired by the greatest movie dunk ever filmed.

Over and over, young Zach watched a videotape of *Space Jam*. In that animated film, Michael Jordan takes off from the half-court line and—as two Monstars try to pull him down—slams it home. Zach was amazed. The VHS tape "would finish, and he would just turn it back on," said his father, Paul LaVine.

From then on, Zach was obsessed with basketball, and he idolized superstar Kobe Bryant. Growing up near Seattle, Washington, LaVine spent hours every day shooting, dribbling, and dunking. Zach, who grew to six-foot-five, often emulated the jams he saw in the NBA Slam Dunk Contests. He earned first-team All-American honors in high school, played one year at UCLA, and then turned pro. As a rookie with the Minnesota Timberwolves in 2014–15, he entered the Slam Dunk Contest—and won.

LaVine wore a *Space Jam*–inspired jersey as he jammed during the 2015 NBA Slam Dunk Contest. He passed the ball through his legs and almost hit his head on the rim.

At that event, LaVine rocked the Barclays Center in Brooklyn, New York. For his first dunk, he reverted back to his childhood. Zach dressed in a white Michael Jordan jersey from *Space Jam* while the movie's theme song boomed through the arena's speakers. While rising, LaVine passed the ball between his legs to his right hand and flushed it on the other side of the rim. His head nearly hit the iron. "I just wanted to come out with a bang," Zach said. "I wanted to show everybody what I got." All five judges, including Julius Erving, scored it a 10.

LaVine finished the first round with another perfect 50. While elevating, he passed the ball around his back to his right hand and then dunked with ease. He thus became the first player in six years to record two 50s in one contest.

The rookie cruised to the final round. For Zach's last attempt, his Timberwolves

In this photograph, Zach's image is reflected in the 2015 NBA Slam Dunk Contest trophy. He joined Kobe Bryant as the only teenagers to win the coveted award.

teammate Shabazz Muhammad tossed the ball off a bar behind the backboard. LaVine grabbed the carom and—while airborne—passed the ball between his legs and dunked. The judges scored it a 49, and LaVine was the new Slam Dunk Contest champion. At age nineteen, he became the event's youngest winner since Kobe Bryant in 1997.

"I'm still on cloud nine," LaVine said. "I feel like I'm dreaming. Seeing all the dunk contests and people hoisting the trophy.... I just saw myself do it and lived it. So it's a dream come true."

Writer Andrew Sharp of Grantland.com declared that LaVine was the game's best dunker since Vince Carter. "[Zach] can already jump 10 inches higher than anyone else, but he's also got the coordination to finish like it's nothing," Sharp wrote. "LaVine is the guy who can finish an alley-oop with a windmill dunk and make it look like a layup. That's what puts him in a category with Vince Carter."

More than just a dunker, LaVine was developing into a terrific all-around player. He averaged 10.1 points per game in 2014–15 and scored 37 in one game. In the early weeks of 2015–16, he ranked among Minnesota's top players, scoring on threes, jumpers, and, of course, effortless slam dunks.

★ GLOSSARY ★

ab muscles—Muscles surrounding a person's midsection, or stomach area; *ab* is short for *abdominal.*

alley-oop—A play in which a player throws the ball up near the rim for a teammate, who catches it midair and jams on the way down.

alumnus—A former student of a school.

baseline—The out-of-bounds line behind the basket.

core—The central part of the body from which the neck, arms, and legs extend.

Division I—The highest level of competition in the National Collegiate Athletic Association.

fast break—When a team races the ball up the court through dribbling and passing.

low post—A nonspecific area close to the basket; big players like to get the ball in the low post so they can shoot a close-range shot.

180-degree dunk—A player twirls halfway around midair before dunking.

power forward—Typically a larger, stronger forward who plays close to the basket.

360-degree dunk—A player rotates all the way around midair before dunking.

tomahawk dunk—A player brings the ball behind his head and then jams strongly as if chopping something with a tomahawk.

top of the key—The top of the circle that's behind the free throw line.

vertical leap—A measurement of how high a player can jump off the ground.

windmill dunk—When a player sticks his arm straight out while airborne then rotates the arm down toward the basket for a dunk.

Books

Aaseng, Nathan. *Michael Jordan: Hall of Fame Basketball Superstar*. Berkeley Heights, NJ: Speeding Star, 2014.

Big Book of Who: Basketball. New York: Sports Illustrated for Kids, 2015.

Christopher, Matt. *Blake Griffin*. New York: Little, Brown and Company, 2015.

Gardner, Robert. *Slam Dunk! Science Projects With Basketball*. Berkeley Heights, NJ: Enslow Publishers, 2010.

Slam Dunk! Top 10 Lists of Everything in Basketball. New York: Sports Illustrated for Kids, 2014.

Wilner, Barry. *The Best NBA Dunkers of All Time*. Edina, MN: ABDO Publishing, 2015.

Websites

Basketball-Reference.com

basketball-reference.com

Includes statistics on every player in NBA history.

Jr. NBA

jr.nba.com

Sections include "Skills And Drills," "About The Game," "Fun Zone," and more.

National Basketball Association

nba.com

Loaded with everything NBA: player profiles, scores, stats, standings, news, and highlight videos, as well as "Kids Club Fun and Games."

★ INDEX ★

A

ab muscles, 37
Abdul-Jabbar, Kareem, 9
Air Jordans, 5
alley-oop, 5, 36, 45
alumnus, 33
American Basketball Association (ABA), 6, 9

B

baseline, 7, 31
Bleacher Report, 14
Boston Globe, 6
Bryant, Kobe, 5, 42, 45

C

Carter, Vince, 5, 26–30, 45
Chamberlain, Wilt, 9
core, 37

D

Dawkins, Darryl, 5, 10–13
Dime magazine, 10
Drexler, Clyde, 5
dunk de la morte, le, 26

E

Erving, Julius, 5–9, 13, 25, 31, 44

F

fast break, 4, 13, 17, 22, 25, 33
Flying High, 18
Fortenberry, Joe, 4

G

Griffin, Blake, 5, 38–41

H

Howard, Dwight, 5, 37

J

James, LeBron, 5
Johnson, Magic, 7
Jordan, Michael, 5, 14, 18, 26, 30–31, 42, 44

K

Kemp, Shawn, 22–25

L

LaVine, Zach, 42–45

N

Naismith, James, 4
National Collegiate Athletic Association (NCAA), 4
NBA All-Star Game, 9, 17, 25, 27, 41
NBA Draft, 13, 16, 23, 26
NBA Finals, 7
NBA MVP Award, 9
New York Times, The, 4

O

Olympics, 4, 26, 29

R

Richardson, Jason, 30–33
Robinson, Nate, 31, 34–37

S

Seattle Times, The, 22
shattered backboards, 5, 12
slam dunk ban, 4
Space Jam, 42, 44

T

technical foul, 4
tomahawk dunk, 5, 41
top of the key, 17

U

USA Today, 27

V

vertical leap, 4, 19, 26, 33, 36

W

Webb, Anthony, 18–21, 37
Wilkins, Dominique, 14–17, 21, 25
windmill dunk, 5, 16–17, 21, 25, 27, 33, 45
Wonder, Stevie, 10